# MY TEACHER CAN TEACH...
## ANYONE!

by W. Nikola-Lisa

illustrations by Felipe Galindo

Lee & Low Books Inc.
New York

Manufactured in China by Jade Productions

Book design by David Neuhaus/NeuStudio
Book production by The Kids at Our House

The text is set in Hank
The illustrations are rendered in pencil, brush pen, rapidograph,
and watercolor on watercolor paper

HC 10 9 8 7 6 5 4 3 2 1
PB 15 14 13 12 11 10 9 8
First Edition

Library of Congress Cataloging-in-Publication Data
Nikola-Lisa, W.
My teacher can teach—anyone! / by W. Nikola-Lisa ; illustrations by Felipe Galindo.— 1st ed.
p. cm.
Summary: An alphabet story in verse about a Latino boy and his remarkable teacher who
can teach an astronaut how to float in space and instruct a ballet dancer how to land with grace.
ISBN 978-1-58430-163-9 (hardcover)   ISBN 978-1-60060-276-4 (paperback)
1. Teachers—Fiction. 2. Occupations—Fiction. 3. Hispanic Americans—Fiction. 4. Alphabet.
5. Stories in rhyme.] I. Galindo, Felipe, ill. II. Title.
PZ8.3.N5664My 2004
[E]—dc22                          2003022904

To the teacher in you, Larissa —W.N.-L.

For Andrea with love —F.G.

My teacher is *so* good,

she can teach . . . *anyone!*

She could teach an Astronaut
how to float in space.

She could teach a Ballet dancer
how to land with grace.

She could teach a Carpenter
how to nail a roof.

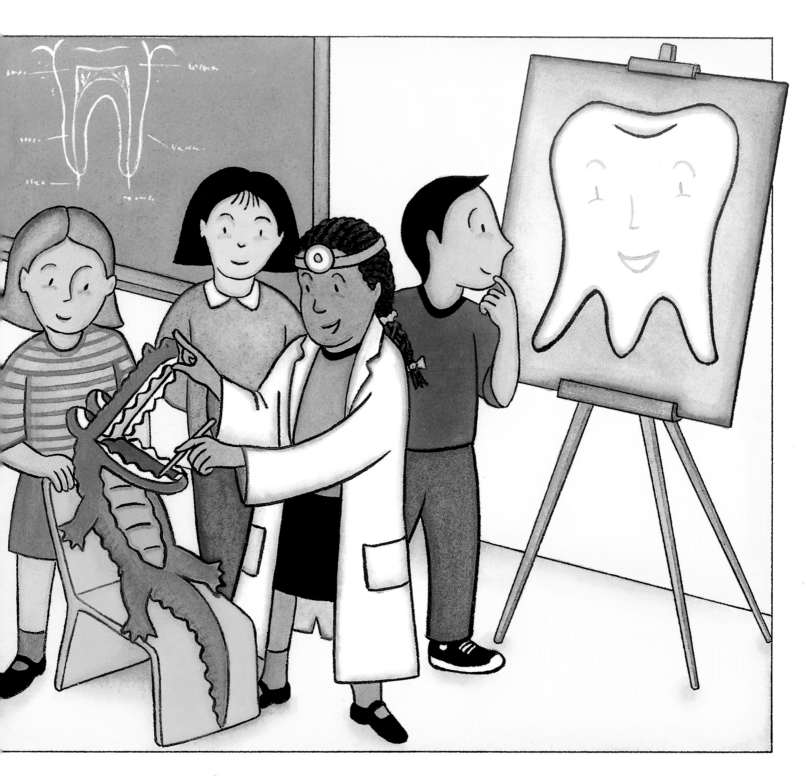

She could teach a Dentist
how to fill a tooth.

She could teach an Engineer
how to dig a hole.

She could teach a Firefighter
how to slide the pole.

She could teach the Governor
how to host a lunch.

She could teach a Heavyweight
how to throw a punch.

She could teach an Illustrator
how to draw a top.

She could teach a Janitor
how to wring a mop.

She could teach a Kayaker
how to pull a stroke.

She could teach a Logger
how to fell an oak.

She could teach a Mechanic
how to change a hose.

She could teach a Novelist
how to write in prose.

She could teach an Opera singer
how to hold a note.

She could teach the President
how to cast a vote.

She could teach a Quarterback
how to throw a ball.

She could teach a Rodeo clown
how to take a fall.

She could teach a Sailor
how to cast a jig.

She could teach a Trucker
how to drive a rig.

She could teach an Umpire
how to call an out.

She could teach a Veterinarian
how to hold a snout.

She could teach a Woodworker
how to build a trap.

She could teach a Xylophonist
how to play with snap.

She could teach a Yodeler
how to sing a mile.

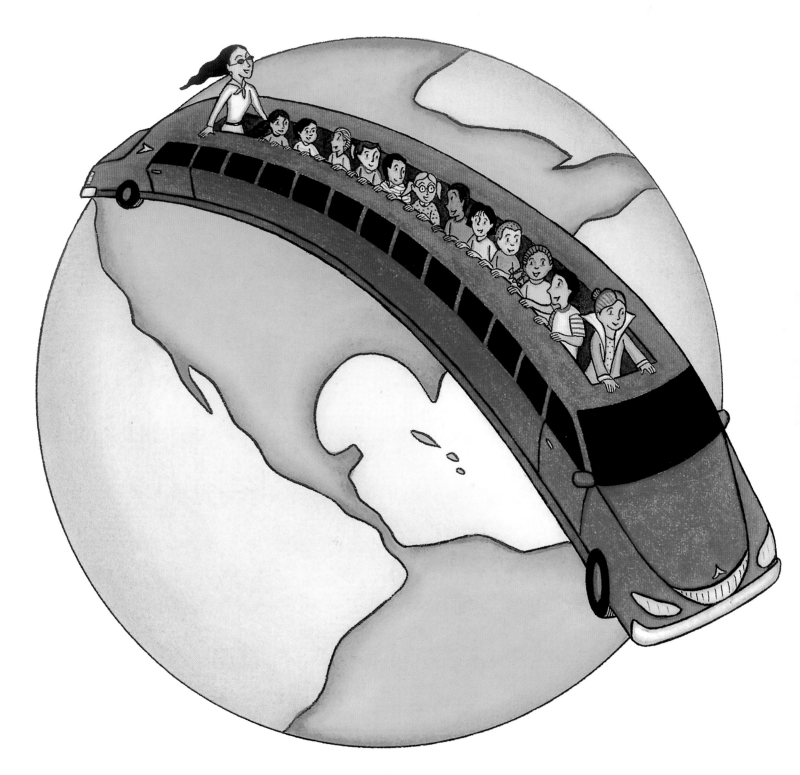

She could teach a Zillionaire
how to live in *style*.